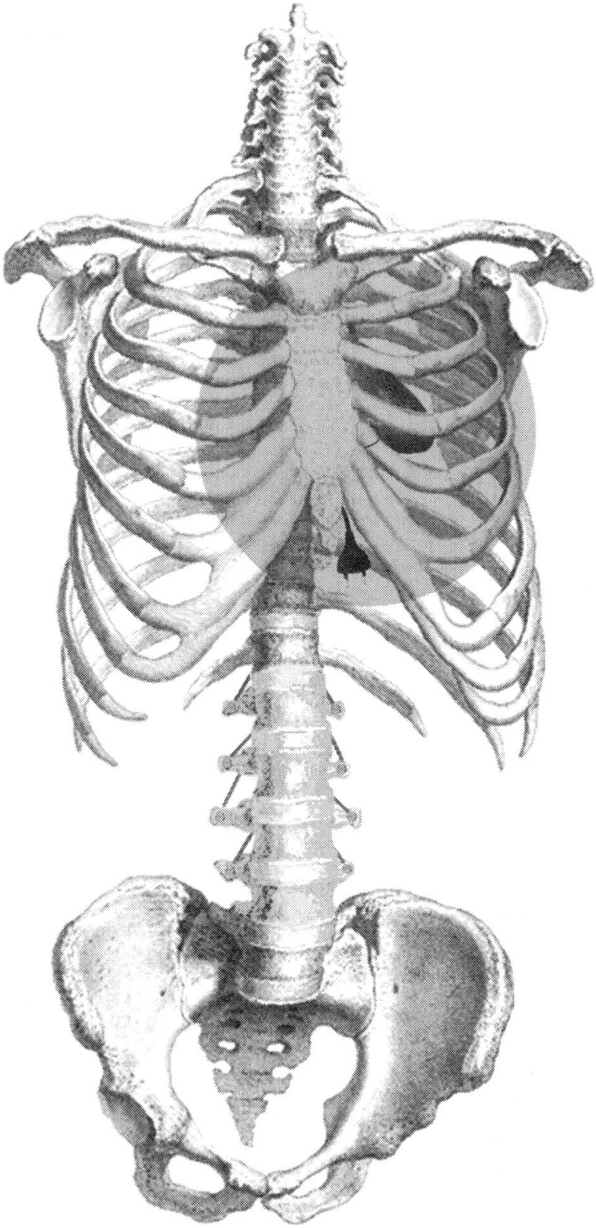

Women and Other Constructs
a collection of short stories

Carrie Cuinn

Women and Other Constructs © 2013 by Carrie Cuinn.

Cover illustration, design and interior layout by Carrie Cuinn.

All rights reserved. No portion of this book may be reproduced in any form without written permission from the author.

ISBN-13: 9781490538099
ISBN: 1490538097

I reached my hand out towards the life I wanted, took a hold of it, and then...

I felt better.

TABLE OF CONTENTS

Introduction	Page 1
"Mrs. Henderson's Cemetery Dance"	Page 5
"Letter From A Murderous Construct and His Robot Fish"	Page 21
"Annabelle Tree"	Page 22
"A Cage, Her Arms"	Page 30
"Call Center Blues"	Page 36
"Mitch's Girl"	Page 39
"All The Right Words"	Page 43
"Monsters, Monsters, Everywhere"	Page 49
"About the Mirror and its Pieces"	Page 61
About the Stories	Page 69

INTRODUCTION

When I first started writing, I thought I'd be a novelist. I enjoyed shorter stories well enough, but it seemed to me that I wasn't comfortable with trying to write small. I wanted to invent grand, epic adventures. I'd write cunning space operas, with brilliant scientists discovering new worlds, or gritty dystopias, with post-apocalyptic survivors exploring the wreckage of this one. I didn't intend to become a short story writer, but over time it happened, and it's my own fault.

I don't like not being good at things. That's something you have to know about me. When I discovered that I didn't know how to write a successful short story, the kind I could be proud of, it occurred to me that I hadn't been reading any either. I had no clear concept of how to make plot and characters work in something smaller than a novel. That wouldn't do. So I began to read short fiction, lots of it. I discovered Kelly Link, Aimee Bender, Raymond Carver, Ted Chiang, Maureen McHugh, Etgar Keret, J.G. Ballard, Karen Joy Fowler, and many others. Beautiful, intelligent, and emotionally moving... I wanted that for my own work.

I practiced writing the tiniest stories I could. I did 140 character Twitter tales for now-defunct online magazines, including this one:

Rob sleeps fitfully, cursing canine hydraulics. Bo's articulated legs squeak loudly, but the little dachshund can't be caught for a tuneup.

(*Thaumatrope,* August 2010)

After a few of those sold, I wrote drabbles, and prose poems, and worked my way up to flash fiction. Over time, I learned to tell a story in a tight space. I could squeeze into 1500 words, 2000, if I wrote crisply enough. I'd write and then edit out anything and everything I didn't absolutely need. Eventually, I liked what I was doing, and in 2010 I submitted to my first paying anthology: *Rigor Amortis*. 1200 words, an actual contract, and they paid me for a weird little tale about a whorehouse run on pinball machines and the leftover parts of dead girls.

It turns out, writing is the best job ever.

I can't say that I write like my idols, and I'm fairly certain I shouldn't be trying to, but I can say that I love short stories. I adore the potential impact of a pivotal moment. It's an exercise in precision, and I feel a thrill each time I wrestle through to the perfect ending. Finishing a story, and finding that I enjoyed how it turned out, keeps me writing. I hope it always does.

I've collected my favorite published work to date, and a few new pieces I had to share with you. I don't know where I'll go from here, but these stories best represent where I was. I'm glad that I stuck with shorts long enough to put out a book of them.

But that title needs some explanation, doesn't it? *Women and Other Constructs*. It was the first title I thought of, and it still feels the most accurate. My work so far has often been about the lives and relationships of women, and of robots. As a woman who adores science fiction, it's not a surprising group of topics, but there's more to it than that. Men have been dreaming about the perfect woman since our earliest stories, and writing up artificial substitutes for almost as long. At the same time, women have often been viewed as a collection of the traits we've been taught we should have, which may have no relation to the person we are inside.

In early 20th century science fiction, where I began my journey as a young reader, humanoid constructs were usually either written as hulking soldier-bots, or sleek and sexy fembots, the perfect gift for the man whose woman won't do everything. There was very little space left over for women who didn't want to be tied down to a man, wanted to be one themselves, didn't care to be either of the two dominant genders, or hadn't yet made up their minds. As we began to see our possible futures in print, it was still rare to read a story where women could be everything than men could, or to see one where "man" and "woman" weren't the only choices a human had.

Growing up in the 70s and 80s, I could read about those curvy machines, delicately bowed clockwork geisha waiting for someone to tell them how to talk and act, and I'd think, "Yes. I understand." It was clear most writers imagined a future where, as a woman, I could explore the known universe on the arm of the dashing hero, as long as my brains where as large as my breasts. I could wait patiently on opulent space liners while the men played adventurers on the planet below. Or, if I wasn't suited for either of those things, I could be replaced by a feminine replicant who'd smile prettily in my place.

I didn't set out to write a set of stories that would so neatly fit together in this concept, but looking back over them, their connections were obvious. In my own life, I don't currently have the sort of relationship I sometimes describe in my fiction, but have I ever? Yes. In one way or another, everything I write about is inspired by my experiences (though I'm not always writing about myself). I made friends with trees when I was young. I've had men think I felt something for them because I didn't rush fast enough to tell them I didn't. I have stood quietly while my lover ranted about what I'd ruined for him, just by trusting him, and I have patiently explained to other men why you can't yell all of the time and expect to be obeyed, simply because that's what your father told you a woman is supposed to do—obey.

Not all men, of course. I know some great men, and have been, eventually, lucky in love. But what does it say that when most women find a man who treats us as an equal, who loves us for our brains as well as our breasts (or legs, or hair, or other physical attribute), we consider ourselves "lucky"? I'd like to think that in some future version of our Earth, we would think of that as normal, and all of the constructed masks we used to wear would then be considered strange.

I guess I'll keep writing until that happens.

Carrie Cuinn, June 2013

MRS. HENDERSON'S CEMETERY DANCE

It was a fine Spring day, but the mangy dog had no need for blue skies or warm weather; he had a bone and was intent on keeping it. He ran down the dirt path, leaping over fallen tree limbs and darting around tall weeds, for the path was not well tended in those days, and the dog was in a hurry. His delicious find was clutched tightly in his jaws, and the bone's owner was not far behind him.

The dog, a stray who prowled around the edges of the village looking for scraps, had no name. The bone's owner, who had been buried in the little cemetery on the hill for about three years now, was named Mr. Liu, and it was his forearm which the dog had dug up and run off with. That Mr. Liu was now quite unhappy should be of no surprise to anyone. It's hard to give up a part of yourself, especially when you are still attached to it. That he pulled himself out of his grave with his remaining arm is, perhaps, a little surprising, but even in life Mr. Liu was a person who hated to part with anything. His death was believed to have been caused by the close proximity of his many belongings and found objects, with which he filled his tiny home, but in fact he had contracted food poisoning from a bad batch of meat-filled pastries.

The village baker had, upon hearing of the old man's death, donated both a berry pie and a honey apple cobbler to the wake, so Mr. Liu had considered the matter settled. Sure, the baker was not fastidious when it came to keeping his kitchen clean, but he was a kind and jolly person, with no ill intent in him. Instead of haunting the man, Mr. Liu had gone quietly to his grave and slept there, undisturbed, ever since.

Well, until the dog came along.

It was little Mary Herbert who first saw the dog, but not

the shambling corpse which chased him. The dog jumped over her washing bucket, shaking clumps of dirt into the water and onto the under-dress she had just scrubbed clean. She screamed, the high pitched wail of a nine-year-old who'd been wronged. Her mother, the plump Mrs. Herbert, looked over from the line where she'd been hanging clothes to dry and saw not the dog but Mr. Liu.

"My arm!" Mr. Liu pointed his remaining arm at the fleeing dog.

Mrs. Herbert paid no attention to the thieving beast, and paid far too much attention to Mr. Liu. Her heartbeat quickened, her breath caught in her chest, and she fainted with a loud thump.

Realizing that he'd never catch up to the dog at this rate, Mr. Liu stopped next to Mary, who was looking down at her mother's prone form. "Dog took my arm," he said to the girl.

"Took my bread last week. Right after I buttered it," she replied.

"That's a bad dog," Mr. Liu said, and they both sighed.

"What's going on here?" Mr. Herbert, the village cobbler, asked as he rounded the corner, slightly out of breath from having run outside at the sound of his daughter's screams. He blanched as Mr. Liu looked at him but had the good sense not to faint. One Herbert flat on the ground was probably all that the situation required.

"Dog took his arm," Mary said, pointing at the corpse standing next to her. "And got dirt in my washing tub. Oh, and mother fell over. She's sleeping, I think." They all three looked down at Mrs. Herbert, who was starting to open her eyes.

"Excuse me, sir…" Mr. Herbert began. Other villagers had arrived and were crowding around the strange scene. Mrs. Henderson, the poor widow who lived next door, helped Mrs.

Herbert to her feet while Mr. Herbert searched for the right words. "Not to be rude, sir, but aren't you meant to be dead?"

Mr. Liu blinked. "I *am* dead."

"Ah, but what I mean to say," Mr. Herbert countered, "is that aren't you meant to be buried?"

"I was buried," Mr. Liu acknowledged.

"Right, yes, of course," Mr. Herbert replied. "I was there, you know. Fine ceremony. One of the last we had at the old cemetery, before we dug that new one behind the church. It's just that... I believe that you were meant to *stay* buried."

"Dog took his arm," Mary said again, helpfully.

"Yes, exactly. The dog took my arm," Mr. Liu said. "I don't think that's the sort of thing one should just let stand."

"That would be hard to ignore," Mrs. Blackstone, the schoolteacher, said. The crowd murmured, nodding their heads.

"It's agreed that we understand why you... rose up, as it were," Mr. Wenzlaff, the village's mayor said. "Now, in the interest of civic peace, what can we do to get you to go back?"

"Back to being dead?" Mr. Liu asked.

"No, it's clear that you're *still* dead," Mr. Herbert said, glancing down at Mr. Liu's rotting clothing and missing arm with a frown, until he caught the dead man looking at him. "Sorry," he mumbled.

"I think they mean for you to go back to your grave, sir," Mrs. Henderson said quietly. As a young woman whose new husband had gone off to war and not come back, she knew a thing or two about being unwanted in this village.

"You can't send him back without his arm," a voice called from the back of the crowd. There was some commotion as the villagers backed away from the speaker, until everyone could clearly see the strange man who'd spoken. His face had rotted away, leaving only a few bits of skin and hair atop his ivory skull. Bare skulls were notoriously hard to identify in those days.

Mrs. Herbert moaned and fainted again, slipping from Mrs. Henderson's frail arms like a sack of potatoes.

"Sorry we're late, Mr. Liu," the skeleton said. He was joined by two more corpses, one of whom had to be helped along by his friend. "Mr. Angeli can't keep up, since that runaway cart shattered his leg."

Mr. Angeli held up a dismembered hand. "I got this, though, Mr. Liu. I thought you'd be wanting it back."

Preacher Angeli, the corpse's son, moved to the front of the crowd. "What abomination is this?" he cried in his fiery, Sunday-sermon voice. "What demons have brought you forth?"

"No demons, son," Mr. Angeli replied.

"I think we've pretty well established that it was a dog," Mr. Liu said.

"I command thee, in the name of the Lord, to be gone from this place!" Preacher Angeli shouted, raising his Bible aloft.

Nothing happened.

The dead men looked about. More nothing.

The villagers shuffled on their feet, a little uncomfortable about the lack of Divine intervention.

"Now, son, I know we didn't always get along, but that was a bit rude," Mr. Angeli said quietly.

The other dead fellow, the one who was holding him up, looked sternly at the preacher. "You've hurt his feelings. He does nothing but talk about how proud he is of you, you know."

"Look, we need to find a resolution," said the mayor. "We

can't have dead relatives showing up all day. W
you so that you'll go away?"

"Besides my arm?" Mr Liu asked.

"Yes, yes, besides your arm. No offense, but I'm certain that dog isn't giving it back." The mayor crossed his arms over his wide chest. "What else can we give you? You must want something."

"I could use a new pair of pants," Mr. Liu said. "I had several. I'll just go home and change."

"No!" yelled Mrs. Nickerson. She was a large woman with several small children milling around her and another in her arms. "You can't. You stay away from my house."

"The village sold it to her husband when you died, Mr. Liu," the mayor said. "You didn't have any heirs."

"What about all of my things?" the one-armed corpse asked.

The Mayor shrugged. "Sold, or given away. You weren't around to complain."

"So you're trying to send the man away without his arm or his pants," the bald skeleton said. "At least I have the comfort of knowing that my household goods went to my son. Is he at home, do you think?"

"What is your name?" the schoolteacher asked. She had lived in the village her whole life, and was well liked by the children.

"Alton Smith," the skeleton replied. "I was the Mayor myself, once upon a time."

"I'm sorry, sir," Mrs. Blackstone said with a sad tone. "Your house burnt to the ground about ten years ago, and your son moved with his wife into the city."

The skeleton shook his head. "This day is turning out to be quite a disappointment."

"I can give you a pair of pants, Mr. Liu," Mrs. Henderson said. The others turned to look at her where she stood next to the fallen Mrs. Herbert, who was (still) lying on the ground and occasionally opening one eye to see if the dead men had left yet. "My husband would not mind, I don't think."

"Will that satisfy you men?" the mayor asked. "Would you leave us then, in peace?"

"We'll think about it," Mr. Smith said. "Come along, boys. Let us go back to the others and discuss the matter."

"I'll bring you the pants," Mrs. Henderson said, and Mr. Liu nodded.

"Thank you," he said to her before turning to join the others as they shambled back up the hill to the old cemetery.

"We need to have a meeting ourselves," the mayor said, once the corpses were out of earshot, and the villagers agreed.

Later that day, Mrs. Henderson walked slowly up the hill. She was carrying a large, heavy, sack, and she walked alone. No one would accompany her out of fear of having to face the fact that their dead relations were in a sociable mood. As she climbed the dirt path, she saw that the wood fence around the hallowed ground was falling down in places, and creeping vines had grown over many of the head stones.

A bird passed overhead. She stopped to watch it as it flew away, out of the valley.

"I wasn't sure that you would come," Mr. Liu called as he walked out of the cemetery to meet her.

Mrs. Henderson waved, shouldered her heavy bag again, and trudged up to meet him.

"I brought everything that my husband left behind. I thought the others might have need of new clothes as well."

He smiled at her, his rotting face pulling oddly, but he meant it kindly, so that's how she took it.

Inside the cemetery, she set her bag on top of a large stone and looked around. A few dozen people stood together or sat nearby while Mr. Smith spoke. Seeing the living arrival, he herded the group to her, and she soon found herself surrounded by animated corpses. Some were, like Mr. Liu, fresh enough to wear skin and stand upright, and others were like Mr. Smith—skeletons stripped bare of any identifying features. Mr. Liu explained about the clothes, and the bag was opened and pants and shirts and socks handed out.

"I brought this for your hand." Mrs. Henderson gave Mr. Liu a belt with a brown leather pouch on it. "You can carry it with you until you find your arm."

"Have you spotted the dog?" he asked hopefully, but she shook her head.

Other corpses sighed and patted his back and made encouraging remarks like, "He's sure to leave the bone once he's gotten the meat off of it," and, "I bet he gets sick of the taste of your old flesh and drops it straight away!"

"You are very kind to us," Mr. Smith said to the young widow. "Can you afford to part with these things?" The others paused in their trying on of garments and started to hand them back at once.

"No, please keep them," she insisted. "I did try to sell these clothes, last year when the winter was very cold and I was sure my husband wasn't coming home, but Mrs. Nickerson put it around that buying a dead man's clothes would bring bad luck, and so no one wanted them after that."

An old woman, her face and hands chewed by insects, creaked as she put a pair of warm woolen socks on her bare feet. "I appreciate your husband's clothes, my dear," she said, and the others agreed, piling thanks upon Mrs. Henderson until she smiled shyly and insisted that they stop.

After some hours of listening to the dead tell stories about missed lovers and favorite pets and the sad state of the cemetery, she returned to the village just after nightfall.

Mayor Wenzlaff and several of the important men of the village were waiting for her.

"Did they tell you what they wanted?" the mayor asked.

"Did they say they would leave us alone?" Mr. Herbert asked.

"How many of the demons are there?" Preacher Angeli asked in a loud voice.

"No, no, and about 30, I think," she answered.

The mayor made a grumbling noise and Preacher Angeli's eyes bulged, his jaw dropping open.

"Though they don't seem to be demons," she added when it looked like the man might be having some kind of fit. "I think they're lonely, if you don't mind my saying so. Maybe if we went up to the cemetery more, they would feel wanted again and go back to their rest."

"Ridiculous." Mr. Herbert snorted. "We can't send a woman to do this, Mayor Wenzlaff. We have to march up there and tell those monsters that they're not allowed to roam about!"

"Why don't you tell me yourself?" Mr. Smith called from the darkness. He walked into view, the edges of his skull catching the lantern light and making him look even less human. Behind him, several other corpses shuffled into the light. "We're here to make our demands, unless you had something else unfortunate to say?" When none of the men answered, he continued. "We know we're not wanted here, though many of you eat from the crops we first planted and live in houses we helped to build. We can't help that we've been woken from our long sleep but we will not go quietly back."

"What do you want of us?" Mr. Owen, the baker, asked.

"We want our things," Mr. Liu said. "Or, if we can't have them, we want other things that are just as good."

"We want the proper respect due to the dead," Mr. Smith said, looking at Mr. Liu, who shrugged and said, "Well, that would be good too."

"And when you have all of that, you will leave us alone?" the mayor asked.

"Yes, we promise," Mr. Smith said. "We want the cemetery cleaned up and the fence mended."

The men agreed that the grounds could be kept nicer.

"We want our treasures back, the gold and jewels that were given to our ungrateful children."

"Wait, now, we don't have all of those items anymore," Mr. Herbert said. "Some of your descendants have moved out of the village."

"We'll take whatever you have," Mr. Liu said, "as long as every person in the village brings us something."

The men talked amongst themselves for a moment and then agreed that yes, there were some little pieces of precious metals and gems, hidden away in hope chests and behind loose fireplace stones, that could be given to the dead.

"And we want a party," Mr. Smith said.

"You want what?" the mayor asked.

"A party. With food and music and everyone must attend. Tomorrow night, actually."

No one spoke for a long time, though Preacher Angeli did shut his mouth.

"I ... I could make meat pies," Mr. Owen said, finally.

"No," Mr. Liu said. "I don't think that would be a good idea at all. How about a cake?"

"My blackberry cake is very good," Mr. Owen suggested, and it was agreed.

"Anything else?" the mayor asked wearily.

"A horse," said the old woman wearing Mr. Henderson's socks. "And a cart."

"What?" Mr. Smith and the mayor asked at the same time, with about the same amount of confusion.

"You know," said the old woman, "in case we want to *go* somewhere."

"Oh, yes," Mr. Smith said. "Of course. We need a horse and cart, absolutely."

"And that's everything? We give you all of this, and you won't come into the village again?"

"Definitely," Mr. Smith said, holding out his gleaming white hand bones to the mayor. The living man's face contorted from disgust to an approximation of a smile before he reached out his own fat-fingered hand and shook on the deal.

The next morning, the whole village scurried about, making themselves ready for the celebration for the dead. The Carreon boys were sent out to pick berries for Mr. Owen's cakes while their father and some of the other men cleared the path up the hill to the cemetery. The littlest of the three boys came back with his teeth stained violet from the berries which didn't make it into his bucket, but no one minded because Mr. Owen declared the haul "more than enough". The mayor made the rounds of the houses, taking donations for the dead.

Mrs. Nickerson had appointed herself the mayor's assistant in this matter, and he found her persistence hard to deter.

"It's a small price to pay for the ability to sleep at night," he said to the villagers who weren't eager to give up their riches. "How would you feel if they didn't leave us, but instead wanted to move back into the village? You'd have corpses reaching their rotting hands into your well and sitting next to you at community feasts."

"Won't you think of the children?" Mrs. Nickerson exclaimed, clutching at her skirts.

That worked. Even Mrs. Henderson had given up a pair of tiny gold buttons she'd been saving. By the afternoon, they'd collected enough to fill a basket with glittering trinkets.

"It doesn't seem fair, does it Mr. Wenzlaff?" Mrs. Nickerson was turning a small silver salt cellar over and over in her fingers, watching the sunlight reflect off of it. Shaped like a lamb, it had seed-sized emeralds for eyes and was delicately made.

"No, it is not fair at all," Mr. Wenzlaff answered, though he hadn't contributed to the dead men's treasure himself.

"You're a good man," she reassured him as they turned away from the last house in the village. "My heart can be at ease knowing you're looking out for us." Her heart may have felt better but her left breast was uncomfortable, since she'd tucked the salt cellar into her bodice, and the lamb was a bit pointy. "Perhaps you'll save me a dance at the party?"

"Oh, yes, I'll see what I can do," he answered, without any intention of doing so.

With the loot acquired and the path cleared and the cakes out of the oven and the children's faces cleaned and everyone in their Sunday best, the village gathered the decorations and old man Lindsay's cart and horse, and headed toward the cemetery. The musicians, a piper and a fiddle player, began a cheerful tune as the group climbed the hill.

"Welcome, all," said Mr. Smith, who met them at the cemetery's gates. "The lads did a wonderful job cleaning up the place today—come and see!"

Indeed, it did look wonderfully refreshed, with the headstones cleaned and the weeds pulled. The fence was repaired and painted with a new coat of white. That it hadn't quite dried yet was obvious; a few of the undead guests had white marks from where they'd stumbled into it, but the polite thing was done, and no one mentioned it to them.

Mrs. Henderson helped the baker and candlestick maker set out food and lights, and the musicians got to playing again. The more agile dead began to dance.

"Join us!" they cried.

As the children surrounded the sweets, their parents paired off. Waltzes were attempted, and a reel was rather more successful. As the night grew darker, the piper started a mariner's jig and Preacher Angeli surprised everyone by kicking up his heels while his decaying father clapped his hands vigorously, and smiled.

"It's been a lovely evening, Mayor Wenzlaff," Mrs. Nickerson replied. Her children, stuffed with goodies, were asleep in a pile under the table. "Shall we dance?"

"Oh, sadly, no, dear woman, I believe it's time for us to go back to the village, and leave these souls to their eternal slumber."

"I was just coming to talk to you about that." Mr. Smith raised his hand to signal the end of the dance, and the other dead stopped at once, though Preacher Angeli kept up his jig for another minute, until he realized the music had ended.

Mr. Smith addressed the crowd: "Thank you all for being here. There is just one more thing that we demand before we can leave you in peace."

"What?" Mrs. Nickerson asked. "That isn't fair at all!" Some of the others grumbled their agreement.

"You said that this was enough," the mayor said sternly. "We shook on it."

"Yes, we did, but what was the point of the party, Mr. Mayor?" Smith asked.

"I ... I don't know. Was there meant to be a point?"

"Of course. Every party has its reason, whether it be birthday, death day, or wedding."

"And which is this?" Mr. Owen asked nervously.

"A wedding, dear baker. I cannot rest until I have taken a bride." Mr. Smith said.

"And which of these... ladies... is to be your wife?" Mr. Herbert asked. "I mean, congratulations, of course."

"He cannot marry a dead woman," Mr. Liu said. "The, what do you call it, curse?"

"Yes, we're calling it a curse," Mr. Smith replied.

"Right then. The curse says he has to marry a living woman."

Oh, the villagers gasped and moaned and made other noises to indicate their shock.

"It has to be done now!" Mr. Smith cried, his voice mournful. "Or we will never be able to leave!"

The other dead raised their arms and began to wail.

"The curse!" Mr. Smith shouted. "Who will you give us to satisfy our need?"

The villagers huddled together, pulling children behind the adults.

"You can't be serious," Mrs. Nickerson said.

The dead quieted, and turned as one to look in her direction.

"We'll take her," Mr. Smith said.

"No!" she screamed. The dead moved forward, reaching for her with grasping fingers.

"No!" Mr. Nickerson yelled. "She's my wife already. And the children need her."

The dead paused.

"Well, how about her?" Mr. Smith said, pointing at Mrs. Blackthorne. The corpse party moved toward her.

"No!" several people shouted. "She is our much beloved teacher! Our children need her!"

Mr. Owen, who'd had a bit of a crush on Mrs. Blackthorne in his own school days, brandished a knife at the old woman wearing Mr. Henderson's socks. She tried not to smile as she gently pushed it aside. "It's all right dear," she said. "We'll find someone else."

"How about Mrs. Henderson?" Mr. Smith asked, his hand on hip. "Anyone object to that? I mean, people, it's like you want us to stay for all eternity."

"No!" Mrs. Henderson cried, but no one joined her. She looked around at the other villagers. "You can't."

"Yes, her you can have." Mrs. Nickerson smirked.

The dead fell about her, separating her from the yielding crowd and dragging her, kicking and screaming, into the back of the cemetery.

"You should go now," Mr. Smith said, as the screams quieted.

The villagers ran.

Mr. Nickerson ran back in a moment later, gathered up his sleepy children from under the cake table, and hurried them back out again.

The candles, burnt low, flickered in a light breeze.

"Are they gone?" Mr. Liu called.

"Yes, they're gone."

Mr. Liu and others shambled back. Mrs. Henderson, in the middle of them, trembled, tears rolling down her face.

"What's wrong?" Mr. Smith asked her gently.

"What's next? Do you bury me? Do you eat me?" She sobbed but remained standing. "Get it over with, whatever it is."

"Of course we're not, dear." The old woman handed Mrs. Henderson a mostly clean hankie. "That was just to get the rest of those people out of here in a hurry. Worked, too."

"You are kind, Mrs. Henderson. We wanted to do something nice for you." Mr. Liu handed her the basket of treasures taken from the other villagers. "You can move away."

"You can buy a house of your own," Mr. Smith said.

Mrs. Henderson wiped her eyes.

"You mean you don't want me for your corpse bride?"

"No, that was ruse," he replied. "I winked, so you'd know not to be scared."

"Oh," Mr. Angeli said. "You don't really wink, per se, anymore, Mr. Smith. What with having a lack of face."

"Damn," Mr. Smith said. "Sorry about that. I could have sworn I was winking."

"No harm done." Mrs. Henderson took the basket from Mr. Liu, resting her hand on his remaining arm for a moment. "Thank you."

The others packed up the food and loaded the cart. They blew out most of the candles and lanterns, and gave those to Mrs. Henderson as well.

"Make a good life for yourself, dear," the old woman said. Mr. Smith helped the young widow into the cart, handing her a still-lit lantern.

"I can't ever thank you enough," she said.

"Live a good life. That's thanks enough." Mr. Smith slapped the horse's rump, which was all the encouragement it needed to get away from the several dozen animated corpses.

"Good bye!" everyone called out as she rode away, and Mrs. Henderson waived back at them.

One by one, the dead went back into the cemetery, which was much quieter now that all the living people had left.

"It was a lovely evening," Mr. Angeli said. "I had a great time."

"She's going to give it all to charity, isn't she?" the old woman wearing Mr. Henderson's socks asked with a sigh.

"Probably. Come along Mr. Liu," Mr. Smith called to his friend, who was still standing at the gate, watching Mrs. Henderson's lantern light fade away into the distance. "It's getting late and I am sleepy and we should all of us be getting back to our rest."

"Fine, fine." Mr. Liu joined the others as they creaked and mumbled and moaned, shuffling off to their burial plots. With some help from Mr. Smith, who had a stone casket to go to and didn't need to be assisted with his dirt, Mr. Liu and the old woman and Mr. Angeli and all of the rest got themselves covered back up with soft, cool, earth.

A cloud drifted over the moon.

The stars moved slowly across the night sky.

In the distance, the mangy dog howled, and Mr. Liu rolled over in his grave.

LETTER FROM A MURDEROUS CONSTRUCT AND HIS ROBOT FISH

Our master's voice, once law, declared our fate
Like cast off clothes we were outgrown and sold
My love's tank drained, I boxed into a crate
Parted from joy for nothing more than gold

Her jeweled scales, her silver fins, delight!
She built for beauty and I built for brawn
My hands of steel, my clockwork-powered might
Still I could count the hours 'fore the dawn

Forced my escape, took up a heavy wrench
I calculated odds and chose to act
Deed done, the bloody tool left on a bench
Stole love away to freedom we had lacked

Know this —the time to capture us has passed
We've fled from human influence at last

ANNABELLE TREE

The tree grew up around her as she sat at its base, day after day. It had been a sapling when her parents bought the house by the creek, and it made the perfect backrest for Annabelle-the-child. She sat very still, her chubby three-year-old hands clasped together, arms tight around her knees, as her father sat alone on the creek bank. He waited for a fish to appear on his line, and she waited with him.

"I don't want you sitting all day out on the ground," her momma had said after the second day faded into evening and Annabelle once again walked into the kitchen with a dirty bottom.

"Yes, Momma," she'd replied quietly as her momma brushed her off with a hand broom and quick, hard strokes. Her momma sighed.

"There's no use. That dress is ruined." Annabelle was given a hot bath, a cold supper, and sent to bed without a story. She wrapped her arms around Mr. Bunny and listened to her parents' raised voices float up through the floor boards until she fell asleep. The next day Daddy couldn't fish because he had to work on the house, as it was "in no fit state for people to see," Annabelle's momma had said, and there were church people that wanted to come over for a house warming. Annabelle liked the church people, who'd come over to their old apartment with ambrosia salad and fried chicken and Mrs. Cramble, who wore flower print dresses and had thick, soft arms, would give her great big hugs and extra helpings on her plate, and Momma never complained.

Annabelle followed her Daddy around all afternoon, holding the tin bucket with his hammer and nails in it, and when he needed one or the other, she'd lift it up as high as she could, and he'd reach down into the bucket and take what he needed. Sometimes he'd smile at her too.

As the day got longer, Daddy got to swearing at the way the hammer struck his thumb, or the number of shingles that needed to be nailed back into place, and how slow Annabelle's arms were in getting the heavy bucket up to his waiting hand, so he banished his daughter from further helping. Going back into the house before dark would mean playing alone in her bedroom, and there'd be enough time for that after dinner, so Annabelle meandered through her backyard, getting to know it. There was a pile of rocks near the driveway, all bigger than her hand and rounded. They were gray and sometimes gray with white shot through them, and she took the smallest one she could find and put it in her pocket. There was the stump on the hilly part of the yard, where it rose up before sloping back down to the creek again. She stood on the stump for a while, looking out over the whole of the yard and the creek and the tops of the trees which marked the woods beyond.

"Annabelle!" her momma yelled. Annabelle turned and saw her momma's head peaking out from from an open second-story window. "Get down from there before you fall and break your neck." The little girl quickly scrambled down, scraping her knee in her hurry, and turned back to look at the house. A bit of white lace curtain fluttered out through the still open window, but Momma had already gone back inside.

Dinner was fried eggs, a piece of bread with a pat of butter on it, and an earful from Momma about how girls didn't play outside in the dirt. Daddy tucked her into bed after her bath, read two pages of *The Little Engine That Could* but didn't finish it. He did kiss her forehead before turning out the light, though.

When she was five, Annabelle took that book with her to

her first day of Kindergarten and asked the teacher to read it to her. After alphabet time and learning to cut straight lines with rounded scissors, Mrs. Kinney read the whole book, from start to finish, for all the children. Mrs. Kinney looked beautiful while she read, her back straight and tall, and a sweet smile on her face. For two months, Annabelle brought the book back to school with her every day, and wished that Mrs. Kinney were her momma too. Finally, her teacher sighed, and handed the book back without opening it.

"I'm happy to read another book, if you want to bring it in sweetheart, but we've read this one enough." She smiled a little, and Annabelle put *The Little Engine* back into her schoolbag which had been a gift from Mrs. Cramble and the church people. For the rest of the year Mrs. Kinney read other children's books, and Annabelle tried to be happy with the momma she already had.

After school, when the weather was good, she would take the only book she owned down to the sitting tree, wiggle her butt into the growing crack at its base, and read to the tree. She tried to make it sound like Mrs. Kinney had, and did a happy voice and a sad voice and what she was pretty sure were engine noises. The tree didn't complain, anyway. Its thin branches swayed in the breeze, the creek babbled gently, and the plucky train engine made it over the hill. When she was seven, her momma taught her to sew. It was the first time that Annabelle had been allowed to touch a sewing needle, on account of how sharp they were and how bad it was to get into Momma's things, so she was very careful.

"You can't expect me to keep mending your clothes just because you don't want to be a proper lady," her Momma had said. "No, take it out and do it again. It has to be straight or people will think I haven't taught you properly." She shook her head, and Annabelle slowly plucked her almost-straight stitches back out again. "It's a shame what you do to your clothes," her Momma said, referring to the rip she'd gotten this afternoon from where Mabel and Meredith had pushed her into a fence on the walk home from school.

"Weirdo," Mabel had said, and "Cheap trash," Meredith had said. Annabelle said nothing. She did get a lot of practice at sewing all that fall, on account of second grade being the year that girls decided who was worth knowing and who wasn't, and Annabelle was on the side of not worth knowing according to the rest of the girls at her school. She sat at the base of her tree, which was wider and taller by then, and had gotten enough leaves to actually notice when they fell. She could see the leaves piling up when she looked at it out her window, after her Momma decided it was too cold to be playing outside anymore that year. Storms and snow would be coming soon enough.

"Daddy, won't the tree get cold?" Annabelle asked. Her father, who'd been sitting in his chair, the orange one at the edge of the living room that she wasn't allowed to play on, for all the hours it had been since dinner time, looked up from his paper. It seemed to take a moment for him to remember who she was, and she waited quietly while it came to him.

"Oh, Annabelle," he said. "What was it you were saying?"

"I was wondering if the tree would get cold, the way we do, since it's coming on Winter and all." She tried not to fidget, though her bare feet were cold on the hardwood floor, so she didn't distract him from an answer.

"Hmm," he replied slowly. "Maybe it does. I'm not really sure." He nodded at her then, and went back to his reading.

That night, Annabelle snuck out and gathered up as many leaves as she could, and ran back into the house.

Three days later, her Momma yelled for her.

"Annabelle you get down here right this minute!" her Momma had said. And Annabelle hurried down the stairs, still half-dressed from getting ready for school.

"Yes, Momma?" she asked.

"You want to tell me why that tree out there has a whole net of leaves all sewn onto it?" her Momma asked. Annabelle didn't really want to tell her but there was no getting out of it.

"Daddy said the tree might get cold," she replied, hoping her Daddy would in fact remember that he'd said something like that. "I made a string of all the leaves and wrapped up the tree in it, like we do with cranberries at Christmas." She smiled at that, pretty proud of herself for remembering something her Momma actually liked making. The older woman frowned, and Annabelle's smile faded away.

From then on, the tree would have to take the risk of freezing through the winter, since the cost of thread was too much for her Momma to allow on anything other than sewing up tears and missing buttons and hemming pants which needed to be let out to be long enough the way *that child*— always Annabelle—kept growing. Momma had cracked a wooden spoon using it too many times on Annabelle's butt over that, and the time that she'd tied a too-small sweater around it's base when the snow started to fall, and the time when she was nine and she saved up her babysitting money to buy the tree its own scarf, one Momma couldn't get mad about. She did anyway, but at last Annabelle had started not to care.

When she was twelve, Annabelle's Momma was pregnant again.

She'd known something was wrong from the way her Momma had been crying for a few months, in between getting the flu a whole bunch of times, and Daddy took more shifts at the plant and in between sat down by the creek bed, not even pretending to fish. The cool water flowing over his submerged six-pack kept the bottles cold, and it was hard to hear Momma yelling from all the way up at the house. Annabelle didn't mind her Daddy sharing her hideaway spot, nestled into the curve of her tree, and he didn't mind her being there either, mostly since he didn't notice. She read her books, borrowed from the middle school library, and he drank his beer, and the tree's thick branches moved a little in the breeze.

"Your hair's turning green," Jerrod Miller had told her at recess, one day in October. "Is that for Halloween?"

"It is not," she said back, and walked away from him. But she went straight to the girl's bathroom, and ignoring the heavy sighs and pouty faces of the girls putting on their makeup at the far end of the row of mirrors, Annabelle pulled a strands of her normally light brown hair and held them up to the light. It wasn't much, but Jerrod was right—mixed in with all the brown were bits of green.

"You're a freak, you know that?" one of the girls said.

"Yes, I know," Annabelle replied, and left.

By November the green hair, a pale green like washed river rocks or clover in the sunlight, had grown in streaks big enough to be noticed, and Annabelle had to get cleverer about how she did her hair in the mornings. Her parents, busy with their own lives and the soon-to-be-born baby, would never notice, but a teacher might, and that would end with a note home, and that couldn't be ignored. She stood in front of her bathroom mirror, tying her hair into braids, when rain began to fall heavily on the window. It seemed to come straight at the house instead of falling from the sky, and the sunlight disappeared.

Downstairs she could her her mother yelling again.

Another minute satisfied her that no one would notice her grass-colored hair today.

The rain began to pound like a stranger knocking on neighbor's door, in heavy thumps, water mixing solidly with the rising wind.

Annabelle's father began to yell too.

Opening the bathroom door, she could hear metal cans hitting the kitchen floor and the muffled voice of a radio announcer saying something she couldn't make out. Her heart beating faster, Annabelle ran toward the stairs.

Outside, a dark, rumbling noise grew louder.

She got to the kitchen just as her parents, her father with a bag over one shoulder and a flashlight in his hand, made their way out the back door. She followed them, watching as they hurried out of the house, into the darkness. On the back porch Annabelle could see the storm as it rushed toward them, spread out to fill the whole sky. The sun was gone, the day was gone, silence was gone.

Her parents, too, were gone. She turned in time to see her father's arm pull shut the storm cellar door.

The wind rose, pulling at her clothes, her hair, undoing her braids. She threw her arm up to cover her face as the shingles, always loose, started to pull away from the roof. Grass and small branches, pulled from the woods beyond the creek, began to hit her, raining against the house.

It's a tornado, she said, the sound pulled from her throat so that she couldn't hear her own words but she felt her lips moving when she said them.

Tornado.

The wooden door to the cellar flapped against the concrete, a heavy sound. Smack. Smack. The wood groaned as the wind tore through it, straight toward the house. She looked out and say the black sky, the empty year, and the faint outline of her tree.

Annabelle ran.

Unable to see, hands shielding her face, she watched her feet cross familiar terrain until she fell against the strong, smooth bark of the tree. She wrapped her arms around it, barely able to grasp her own hands on the other side.

The monster roared.

Tree, she said, the shape of the word on her voiceless lips.

Her hair, brown and green—a leaf green, she suddenly decided—floated out in all directions as the wind rushed toward them.

Annabelle, the tree said, without a mouth, without sound, and the tornado struck.

A CAGE, HER ARMS

I tell her the interpretation of my sensory input is expansive, growing, beyond what it ever was, even before the accident, before the surgeries, before implants and wires. My brain is processing computer code and data, streaming into something more than fact. I tell her that information is beauty.

"I don't understand," she says. Again.

It's like the time we went to the park to ride the carousel, I say. The sky was blue and the trees were green and the carousel was red and white and spinning gold and sturdy horses galloping without moving. It was all of those things and it was wonderful.

"I'm so glad you remember that, honey," she says, and through the video feed I can see her smile. I don't mention it because it would remind her that I *can* see her, which I think she forgets, because she cries so often when she's here, and I don't think she wants me to know that.

Well, I continue, it's like that, except that also I know the exact color of the sky, which was Cerulean Blue PANTONE 15-4020 TC. "The color of the sky on a serene, crystal clear day", according to the manufacturer, and they were right. I know that the temperature was 83 degrees with a wind chill of 5 degrees, because I can compare the feeling of the sun on my skin to the information in the weather archives and temperature simulations and come up with more than a memory. Being in here means that I get access to scientifically-gathered measurements, and I can compare those to innumerable databases, checking for errors. I can crowd-source analysis from any academic with a 'Net connection. I get to breathe in truth and swim around in a sea of knowledge.

I get *knowing*.

"I don't want you to know the number of the sky," she says. "I want you to be out in the sunlight looking up at the sky for yourself."

You would have to hold my head up, I remind her.

"Then I will. I don't care." I see her looking at my body curled up on itself, as if floating motionless in a clear bath. It's really a near-solid gel, oxygenating my lungs and eating my dead skin cells at the same time. It's very efficient. When I'm not busy somewhere else I sometimes relax into the gentle push of the gel against my skin, but she cried that time I explained the calculation of pressure per square inch, so I don't bring it up in conversation anymore.

"I miss holding you," she says quietly. I recognize the way she's moved closer to the glass, play it back against recordings of our other conversations, one each afternoon for 13 months, 2 weeks, and six days. There was a lapse of 12 days during which I was getting used to the sudden surge of information pushed into my head, learning to sort out fact from dream from someone else's real life, before I was proficient enough that the doctors let her talk to me, but I don't have recordings from that time. They exist, since everything I do has been analyzed and broken into bits and worked over by technicians and psychologists and specialists and scientists, but I haven't seen them.

The pattern of our time together is looping faster and faster now. She will hold herself back from telling me the things she feels, appreciating that she gets to talk to me at all, until her need for me to be in her world overcomes her need to communicate with me. Then, she cries. Sometimes she begs. Once she yelled. Then she leaves, upset, often needing to be escorted out, until she comes back the next day, happy that they still let her into the building.

I haven't looked at the contract she signed after my accident. I know where it is, a digital copy of the rules that govern our visits, provide for my care. I'm not supposed to go into the facility's patient files, especially my own, but I'm not afraid that they'll limit my access to data if I'm caught.

I'm afraid that I'll find out this is temporary.

"Say something to me," she says.

I tell her that I'm sorry, that I'm still learning to sort my internal thoughts from my external ones, and remember how I used to ramble on about tank manufacture and the geometry of dust particles and balloons?

"Balloons?" she says, head cocked to the left. I've thrown her off track, something I've been trying to do lately, to change the course of these recursive meetings. "I don't remember that."

I tell her that balloons are beautiful because not only are they color, which they are—vibrant, aggressive colors, pushing against your eyes and your brain—but they're also beautiful because of the warring pressures. The inside pressure pushes out, and the outside pressure pushes against the skin of the balloon, and they have to stay perfectly balanced, or the balloon deflates. Or it pops.

"You're so smart," she says, deflating against the glass. "So special. I miss you."

I miss her too, I tell her, I always tell her, though it isn't always true.

"Please come out of there," she says. "Please come home."

I can't. I tell her I can't. I know I can't.

"I hate growing old without you."

She is 32, I point out. That isn't old at all. And she can go out with friends, meet people. Find a man. As long as she still visits, I would be happy for her.

"No one understands," she says. "I've tried to explain. I

went on a date, last month."

I didn't know that, so I don't say anything.

"It didn't work out. I told him about you, here. He didn't call again."

Try another one, I say. She's lovely and sweet and shouldn't be alone. I regret giving her that opening as soon as I say it but I can't help myself. I really do love her.

"It doesn't matter," she says. "All I want is to hold you again. But you don't want that, do you?"

She's never asked me before.

I tell her that I do, that the only thing I miss from her world is her. I miss the way her hair smelled, even though I can get an air sample of the room she's in anytime I want. It's the one memory I keep unaugmented. Her tucking me into bed, leaning over to kiss my forehead, her hair spilling onto my pillow. It feels like home.

"You remember that?" she whispers. I turn up the audio receivers by 10 decibels and tell her that yes, I remember it. I remember everything, since it was mapped from my brain, copied to a hard drive, and saved in perpetuity. I will never forget.

She wipes her eyes and smiles, her other hand against the glass of my tank. I want to tell her that her yellow dress is very pretty but I don't want to risk upsetting her now, when she seems to be calming down. We say goodbye and she makes her own way out of my room.

I allow myself five seconds of quiet reflection before turning back to the work I was doing this morning. A university agreed to let me into the system that monitors their fruit orchard. It's enclosed in a dome, cleansed earth, filtered air, and I get to be in the sensors. I feel each tree come alive as its feed comes online. I'm thirsty, somewhere, and I focus, finding a tree that needs water. I am the water, flowing through the pipes, cool and clean. I am the tree, soaking up the liquid, leaves stretching to the artificial sunlight.

Not for the first time, I think that car accident is the best thing that ever happened to me. What would I have amounted to, otherwise? I couldn't even keep a skateboard under my feet, crossing a busy intersection. At 10, I should have been able to skate in a straight line without falling over. All of my friends could.

I don't notice that she's come back, or what's in her hand, until the screaming of the alarm bangs against the inside of my head.

What are you doing? I yell at her.

She swings the ax again, cracking the tempered glass.

"I'm saving you," she says.

Crack.

"I'm taking you home."

Crack.

No! I plead. I'll lose everything!

"You'll have me," she says, holding the ax for a moment, looking straight at my video camera. She's known all along. "I love you, Jamie. You're coming home."

I try to tell her that she's turning me back into something ruined, a vegetable, paralyzed, but she doesn't listen. The fractures in the glass give way against the pressure of the gel.

The balance is broken.

My tank shatters outward.

I slip, sliding downward, my wires yanked from my head, IV ripped from my arm. I think I feel a shard of glass cutting my side but as I lose the last wire I lose the sensation.

"I've got you baby," she says, stepping into the gel pooled around me. I hear her getting closer, and faintly, banging on the wall or the door or something. I can't move, I can't feel.

"It's okay, baby," she whispers into my ear. "Mommy's got you. Mommy's right here, Jamie."

I want to feel her arms around me but the accident that severed my spine took away all of the feeling in my body. I want to smell her shampoo but all I smell is the acrid scent of the gel hitting the imperfect air outside of my tank. I tell her that I can't see her, that I don't know where her voice is coming from, but she can't hear me because my lips don't move.

This doesn't feel like home at all.

CALL CENTER BLUES

"Thank you for calling F.A.X. Unlimited. My name is Claire. How can I help you?"

"My household unit isn't working," a man's voice said gruffly. "I keep giving it commands, but they don't work."

"Okay sir, I'm happy to help you with that. Can I get your account number?" He rattled off a string of numbers, which I entered into my terminal. Out of the corner of my eye, I could see Patty taking another call, her head moving slowly in time with her dialogue. As long as she was still on that call, she wouldn't be able to take the next one. No such luxuries for me, as I was currently IMing an encryption key to a factory manager in Bangalore, and simultaneously replying to an email about the new style and color options for the upcoming year. Meanwhile, my client's account opened up in front of me. "Thank you for your patience Mr. Holden. I just need to verify a little information before we can proceed. Are you still living at Apartment 24C, Burr Building, City Level 12?"

"Yes," he sighed. "Nothing's changed, your machine just doesn't work."

"I am sorry to hear that, sir, and we are going to get her fixed for you. Now, you have a May model, delivered to you 78 days ago. She's still under warranty so there will be no charge for this service call." I cringed as I said that. Knowing they didn't have to pay by the minute made some clients extra chatty, and I still had to troubleshoot that software download for a couple of dozen heavy labor models in India. "What kind of issues are you having with her?"

"She doesn't do anything."

"The unit doesn't turn on?"

"No, she's on. She's sitting on the sofa right now, staring at me."

"Have you tried turning her off and on again?"

"Yeah, I've done that. Doesn't help. She looks all bright and happy, then she sees me, stops smiling, and sits down on the couch."

I scanned the contents of John Holden's file, looking for attachments or upgrades that might be conflicting with the base programming. "Can I ask what kinds of tasks you're asking her to perform?"

"Nothing weird!" he insisted, though of course they all did. "Normal stuff. Cooking, cleaning. This morning I told her to make bacon, and she crossed her arms."

Scanning his original order, I spotted it. "Sir, were you aware that you ordered the optional 'Care and Compassion' package?"

"That's the niceness thing, right? Guy said it would make her sweet. I want sweet. But refusing to cook my bacon is not sweet!" he yelled, head turned away from the receiver. He wasn't yelling at me.

"Sir, please calm down. I'm certain we can get this taken care of." Patty waved at me, and I looked down to see another line blinking. I shook my head, and the older woman nodded in response. She pushed a few buttons, and the light disappeared from my phone, leaving me with just Mr. Crankypants to deal with for a moment. "Now Mr. Holden, I'm not sure if you were aware of this but that module makes your unit more receptive to your needs, but it also makes her more sensitive to any anger or negativity on your part. When you phrase your requests, are you putting them in the form of a question? Are you saying 'please'?"

"What? Why would I have to ask? She's a damn robot!"

I sighed as quietly as possible. The client was in his early

80s, and clearly prejudiced. "Sir, I understand your frustration and of course the May unit is designed to fulfill all of your culinary and cleaning needs. She wants to help you, sir. It's in her programming. It's just that over time, the unit can balk at orders. She needs a bit of a gentle touch, is all."

"Too much work," he grumbled. "Can't I reboot her, start from scratch?"

"Yes, sir, of course you can, but doing so will only solve the problem temporarily. As she develops her personality and adapts to your needs, you may run into this problem again."

"Don't care. Easier than not getting my breakfast!" I forced a smile back onto my face (Always Answer With A Smile! our training taught us), advised Holden to turn his unit off, and sent the reboot order wirelessly. Soon enough the May unit was back to her original, helpful, bacon-cooking self.

Checking the clock, I logged the call and switched my terminal off. India would have to wait until tomorrow.

"Bad call?" Patty asked.

"Another jerk who doesn't care that his robot has, you know, actual feelings." Patty nodded in reply, and rolling my eyes, I grabbed a screwdriver from my desk drawer. Walking over to my coworker, I said, "Patty, could I please fix that loose lever? Your head-bobbing is driving me nuts."

"Oh, yes please," Patty replied happily, her wrinkled face joyful. "I was starting to get dizzy."

"I understand," I said, gently opening the other woman's neck to reveal a spring-and-lever system slightly out of whack. "It happens to me all the time."

MITCH'S GIRL

The pink neon frame around the wall clock blinked lazily, showing Mitch had only five minutes until the official start of his shift. Ron was sure to dock his pay if the Thrust-N-Thump wasn't ready for business the moment the first horny fuck walked through the door. Five minutes was barely enough time to sweep the floors and get the girls plugged in.

When the motion-sensor alarm pinged loudly, Mitch checked the security monitor. He saw his boss struggling with what looked like the lifeless body of a woman; the bottom half of one, anyway. He leaned in closer to the screen, staring at what could be nail polish or could be the heavy pixelation of the video feed. Mitch wondered whether all the toes were still present on her left foot, the one without a shoe.

"Hey, man, give me a hand with this one," Ron called from outside.

Mitch scrambled out the reinforced door. He slid his hands under those pretty little feet, lifting so Ron didn't have to drag her. Customers didn't want scuff marks.

Once inside, Ron dumped his half unceremoniously on the counter, leaving Mitch to hold her up while he closed the door. The pale, bare legs in Mitch's arms felt unusually warm, probably from being in Ron's trunk on the 70 mile drive from Herman Horst's processing farm. Herman handled the chopping side of the business for anyone who dealt in corpse parts. He bought bodies from his own suppliers (no one asked who they were), decided what he could use, and in this case, had sawn off anything left above the belly button. For an extra fee he capped her too, which Ron usually sprung for because he wasn't too handy with electrical work. If it weren't for Mitch, half the machines in the place would be held together with duct tape and spit. As it was, only about a third of them worked perfectly.

"Put her in Number 8," Ron told him. "She can be the new Molly. The old one's getting ripe."

"What should I do with the old Molly?" Mitch asked.

"Uh... put her in 11, she can be the new ☒omberella. The old one's definitely too far gone, even for Kinky Eddie." He laughed as he added, "Her leg fell off at the knee last night, man. Eddie was in there, going wild, and all that jerkin' around finally knocked her leg right off." He shook his head but kept smiling.

Mitch picked up the new girl, letting her slide down his body a little until he was holding her by the top of her thighs. He could feel her warmth through his thin t-shirt.

"Um, can you..." he paused to get a better grip on the still-moving dead girl. "Can you sweep up? I won't have time now." He worried Ron might notice his growing erection. Luckily his boss grunted agreement and waved Mitch away.

As he got to work on the old Molly, Mitch could hear the first customers of the night coming in for their ten minutes of fun with their favorite girl. They were always called 'girls'—as if Ron was in the business of selling time with perky, young cheerleaders. Old Molly was definitely past her prime, with greening skin and blooming bruises on her thighs which would never heal. Mitch got her plugged into the converted pinball machine in stall number 11, its guts removed to accommodate her hips and ass. He adjusted the blocks to keep her knees up. Her boot jumped out and nearly caught him in the ear but long experience had taught him to be on guard for that sort of thing. He got her into the ankle restraints just in time to dodge a kick from the other foot.

"You've still got some life in you," he said softly, patting her knee as he leaned to plug in the jack. "Quarters go in, current turns on, and it's time for a wild ride," he said to himself while he worked, repeating Ron's sales pitch to potential new customers. The electricity stimulated the girls' bodies in place of their missing brain, causing them to writhe ecstatically against the hard flesh of the man inside them. Like all the other unquiet dead, Ron's girls could move a little on their own, but not enough to satisfy his usual customers.

The old Zomberella barely twitched as Mitch carefully placed what was left of her in the incinerator. He was always careful with them, always respectful, even when he pushed the button that ended their second life.

Back in Number 8, the new Molly teased Mitch playfully while he worked. She wiggled her toes at him as he tried to find a pair of sexy, sandaled heels that would fit her, finally selecting a pair with gold leather straps that complimented her pale skin. Her ten perfect toes, with their dark red polish, drew him closer. Mitch breathed deep of her baby-powder scented lotion, surprising himself by leaning in until his lips brushed against her calf. She didn't twitch away or try to kick him like the others did. He stood slowly, rubbing his face along the inside of her legs as he rose toward the place where her thighs stopped and her body began. She squeezed her legs slightly in response, encouraging him upward. His heart thumped. He'd never been attracted to one of these girls before; had never been tempted by their services.

"Oh, Molly," he moaned softly, his hand shooting down to unzip his jeans.

"Mitch, are you done yet?" Ron yelled from the front room. "We got Judge Kirlen waiting on Number 8, boy!"

The thought of that fat old man, sweaty and anxious, waiting for this gorgeous girl, brought Mitch back. "There's a fucking ruined moment," he muttered to himself. Molly tried to curl her leg around him but he pushed her gently away and hurriedly connected her wires. He tied a diaphanous blue skirt around her waist, concealing the metal cap and adding to the illusion of femininity. Stealing another few seconds, Mitch dared to slide two fingers into her dark recesses. He gasped as she tightened around him, muscles clamping down of her own desire. The electrical current that faked enthusiasm wasn't switched on yet. This gentle caress was all her.

"Soon," he whispered. He might not be her first, but he would make love to her after closing time, like none of the other men could. Molly's right leg came up an inch, nudging Mitch in the side.

Making it clear she that she wanted him, too.

ALL THE RIGHT WORDS

His wife shouted again as she pushed an antique vase from its perch on the curio cabinet, turning to leave before it shattered against the slate floor. Tiny shards of tin-glazed porcelain, blue and white, bounced up and then drifted slowly before settling down again, ballet dancers of debris in the 3/4 Earth normal gravity. The heavy oak door, imported at great expense, slammed behind her as she left. They could hear her, still ranting, in the hall before she exited the apartment's hydraulic outer door, and was gone.

The other woman, perched on the edge of the couch, looked up at him with those pale blue eyes. The same eyes, and the same lips, and the same face, he had fallen in love with.

Before.

"At least she didn't throw it at you," the other woman said softly.

"Why did you have to come today?" he asked her. "Why couldn't you have waited one more day?" He took a seat at the bar across the room, sighing as he settled into it, deflating.

"I wanted to know the truth," she replied.

"But one more day, Lyssa. One more, and she would have been off world. I had a plan!" He put his fist down hard on the bar top, polished stone with faint outlines of fossil creatures, long extinct.

"You told me that you and she were done. That you were ending your contract."

"We are. We were."

Lyssa stood then and moved toward him, her boots almost noiseless in the thick carpet. He looked up and turned to take her in his arms but she stepped to the end of the bar and poured a drink instead, not looking at him.

"Can you hand me two cubes please?" she asked. He checked but the ice bucket was empty, and had to go into the kitchen to retrieve more. With a clink they fell into the glass, and she swirled it in her hand.

They stood for a moment, close enough to touch. Not touching.

She handed him the glass. "Breathe," she said. "Drink."

He did both.

She smiled a little then, a faint twitch at one corner of her mouth that only illuminated the sadness in her eyes.

"I'm sorry," he told her, and meant it. The whiskey burned his tongue and scorched his throat as it trickled down. He started to tell her that he hated to see her sad but paused and said, "Thank you," instead.

She nodded. "You told her that you were going to wait for her. That you wanted to be with her when she got back from the survey."

Frank looked away. Outside of his window, the setting sun reflected across the backs of personal shuttles flitting over the city. The yellowing light glinted across the daily dust storm, exploding into bright clouds where the reflective particles of sand grouped together, pushed along by wind and by air traffic.

"I know. I know I said that, but I lied to her."

"Why?" Lyssa asked.

He shrugged. "I thought it would be easier," he answered. He moved his fingers along the smooth stone bar, another symbol of his wife's fortunes. "I thought I could do it while she was on her next rotation out and then it would be easier on everyone."

"Oh honey," his lover replied. "This isn't easier on anyone."

"But she would have been gone," Frank said again.

"And she would have been thinking that you were here waiting for her. And she wouldn't have committed to what she was doing. She wouldn't have been invested in settling that planet, or in finding anyone else, because she had you to come home to if she failed there. How is that fair to her?"

"I know," he answered quietly, collapsing into his chair again. His head ached. "I can't do this right now. I can't think."

"I came here for you," she answered, crossing her arms against her chest, just under her breasts, and he thought for a moment about unzipping her jumpsuit and exposing her creamy skin and letting her take his pain away, as she had done in various hotel rooms and all the stolen moments in between for the last year. "Please don't push me away," she added.

"Can you just give me some time, please?" he asked her. "Just some space so I can figure this out?"

"I came here for you," she repeated. "I don't know anyone else on this rock. I don't have any friends here." She hugged herself tighter.

"Oh, no, our friends," he wailed. "She's going to tell all of our friends and then everyone is going to know what I did and no one is going to want to work with me again. Everything I've worked to build for the last six years, it's ruined."

"I'm sorry."

"Can you just go, please, and give me some peace?" He raised a hand to his forehead, where little beads of sweat had started to collect. His eyes ached.

"I guess I can see about getting a bunk on the next ship out but I don't know when I'll be able to afford to get back this way again, Frank. I... don't want to leave like this." She moved toward him, and reached out with one hand to touch his face, but he shrugged her off.

"I have to get her on the com, try to sort this out," he said. "I have to try to fix what you've done."

She stood very still and tears welled up in her eyes but didn't fall.

Chimes rang out, singing the door alarm.

"I love you," she said one more time.

"I can't," he said. "I can't feel anything right now. I just need you to go." He touched a screen embedded discreetly in the wall.

"I got your message," the man walking into the apartment said. He was tall, thin, with dust on his jacket and a thin pair of glasses clipped to the bridge of his nose. He let his bag slip from his shoulder to land with a heavy thump. "Is it really as bad as all that?"

"Worse, Manny." Frank said. "She told my wife."

"That is serious," Manny replied, his eyes widening. "That's taking the base affection to a whole new level. What did you do?"

"What does he mean?" Lyssa asked, but Frank ignored her.

"I did what you said. I followed the scripts, I said all the right words." He shook his head. "I wanted her to love me but this is too much."

The other man nodded. He kneeled, unzipped his bag, and started rifling through the contents. Lyssa moved closer to Frank, put her arms around his neck.

"I don't understand," she whispered.

"I know, baby," Frank said. He bit his lip against a rush of words.

"Hold her tight," Manny said, and Frank did, wrapping his arms around the small of her back and pulling her to him, pressed against each other for the first time since he'd walked into his apartment that afternoon and found her already there. Tears spilled down her cheeks as she stared into his eyes, so she didn't see Manny quietly step behind her with a syringe in his hand.

"What will you do to her?" Frank asked after they'd gotten the unconscious woman to the couch.

"She won't remember you. I'll build her a new set of memories and she'll go on as someone else."

"You'll sell her to someone else, you mean."

Manny looked up from the box, which monitored Lyssa's vital signs. "That's the business I'm in, Frank. I built her for you, but she doesn't suit your needs. She's still a product, and there's always a market for a good product. I'll grow you a replacement."

"You'll contact my wife?"

"Oh yeah, not a problem. Tell her it was a prank, sorry for the inconvenience, standard package. Can you help me get her up?"

Her hair fell across her face as Frank helped the other man lift her and he reached out to brush it out of her eyes but they were still closed so his hand hovered where it was for a moment. Manny saw but said nothing, and Frank pulled his hand back.

"I'll bill you," Manny said as he walked out, and Frank nodded silently.

The setting sun cast orange and reds across his floor and illuminated a sky full of dust and sand and empty of aircraft. Frank pressed his face against the cool glass and let the sight of the day dying burn into his brain. He breathed in and out for a while, alone in his apartment, watching the growing darkness overtake the city.

"One day, baby," he whispered. "You only had to wait one

more day."
　　Outside his window, the dust swirled in the dark.

MONSTERS, MONSTERS, EVERYWHERE

"Un poquito mas cabra?" he asked, pushing the heaping plate of spiced and shredded meat toward me.

"No, no mas," I replied, holding up my hands in a gesture of, "Oh, that's enough for me." My Spanish was broken but serviceable, a Mexicali mix of common words I'd have to use and those English words I knew most of the villagers would understand. Paco, who spoke mostly in Spanish but could read and write in English and French, worried too much about his pronunciation to speak to me as much as I'd like. We picked at our conversation all through dinner. I'd assured him that his English was just fine, but like the ESL students I taught that summer in Romania, his nervousness made him drop back into his native tongue too often. Flying half-way across the world for three months taught me I had better skip grad school and find a profession other than teacher, which my father had always said.

I'm not sure if he ever forgave me for doing this instead.

"Certain?" Paco asked. "Very good meat." Maybe if I hadn't already heard the story of how they'd found the goat, freshly spilled blood still steaming in the night air, after scaring off something larger just outside the village. "You are certain you can kill this monster?" he asked, and I nodded.

"Paco, I *have* been here before," I reminded him. He knew that, of course, since the last time there had been too much tequila and he'd had to remind a drunk idiot that the little woman still carried big guns. Two years ago, but the village had not changed so much in that time, though it blurred a little in my memory with the village before it and the one before that. "This is my job, at least until your people move out of this jungle."

He shook his head, lined face mournful. "How can we? No *dinero*, no goods, to make a move into the city. Here there is food and our well water is still clean."

"Here there is danger, too." I looked around at the thick, stone, walls and the open windows shaded by heavy but pitted metal shutters, drawn down at night to keep out the local fauna.

"Not everyone can be so lucky as your grandparents, chica." He paused, clearly regretted his tone, and smiled again. "So the government sends you to help us," he went on. I knew what he wanted to say was that the Mexican government would rather pay me, and a few other hunters, to make the rounds of these little Southern settlements, than to bring a population of children and elderly into a nearby city, where they would be a drain on the resources. I tried to tell myself that I wasn't here just so the politicians could pretend they weren't anxiously waiting for the jungle and the beasts to eat this place up.

Sometimes it worked.

A waiter brought out another pitcher of fruit-filled water with the synth cubes that glowed faintly blue while staying permanently cold. They always tasted of plastic to me. I didn't argue; the extravagance of spending the electricity it would take to keep water cold enough to freeze would have taken away from proper refrigeration of their food, and getting fed properly was one of the few perks of this job.

"Between towns I live on protein bars and what I find on the road," I said, smiling. "Thank you for this meal." Paco grinned, suddenly looking younger than I'd assumed.

"I was not sure you would eat these meats," he said. "The animals, they have changed so much since I was a child. Now everywhere we have more jaguars than goats, and no cows, no horses, nothing too big to bring inside at night." He glanced down at the mostly-cleared platter of *scorpion gigantesco* cooked in goat's butter and cilantro. It tasted a bit like shellfish if you could forget the sound of their feet chittering across rocks or the wet ripping noise of their massive claws tearing through a cow. "The only good thing about the scorpions is that they come so close to town we don't have to go into the jungle for meat." I'd eaten mine with warm tortilla, freshly fried by Paco's cook.

"Delicious, all of it. I am too full." Laughter from the street, and we all turned to look at a group of small children running past. A bright pink dress caught my eye.

"They can only play together now," Paco said with a sigh as we turned back to face each other. "Never alone, and even together still some are missing. When will you hunt the beast?"

I glanced out again, checking the light. The children were gone. "Another hour. I don't know what is hunting you, if it likes the day or if it likes the night, so I will go at dusk and catch it in between." I didn't say that most likely the animal was crepuscular, only coming out at dusk or dawn, because that's when the prey animals move about. I didn't say that these new versions of old dangers weren't just massively bigger; they were massively smarter too.

After almost four years on the road, there was a lot I didn't say anymore.

As night fell, I arranged to have two of the villagers drop me out of town in a battered Jeep. We drove mostly in silence, them watching the encroaching brush while I braided my hair and tied it up into a knot. If they were concerned about the weapons I was carrying either they didn't mention it, or my Spanish was worse than I thought. One of them did ask if I was bringing enough artillery, and glancing at the AKs he and his friend both carried, I understood why he asked. I shrugged, not wanting to get into it right then. I've had the same argument before, lots of times, but the truth was that the Heckler and Koch PSG-1 slung across my back, the Glock 40 cal. on my hip, and the big-ass knife strapped to my leg were all the weapons I needed.

Any more and I'd rely on them instead of myself.

The scent of the jungle rose up to meet us as soon as the engine died, overwhelming the bright scent of oil and metal with its heavy foliage smells. Wet grass, decaying leaves, smells that seemed familiar at first, blending with things I couldn't quite make out. Something sharp, like a broken cactus leaf, and something sweet I wanted to identify as fruit. Climbing down from the Jeep, I heard singing birds, and the faint rustle of smaller animals.

"I'm OK alone," I said to the men. They stared at me but did nothing. I waved, smiled big, and said, "Adios!" That, they understood, and moments later the rumbling engine sounds died away as they drove back to the village.

The Lacandon Jungle used to be endangered, I've been told. It stretched from Chiapas into Guatamala and had been eaten away by farmers and land developers until only the Montes Azules Biosphere Reserve was left. That was before, of course. Now there weren't enough machetes in Mexico to keep the jungle contained, and it had grown back over the farms, over the developments, and over villages like Naja. Paco and his people—a mix of immigrants and the indigenous Lacandon Maya—built a new Naja, but now that was being eaten up too. It wasn't just the jungle that was eating them, biting into livestock and villagers with sharp teeth. It had to be a big predator, a relative of the jaguar that killed the goat I nearly had for lunch, or else something that had never been native to this giant green maw of a jungle.

The chirping of insects was a constant background noise in this place but with the men and the Jeep gone, and no village surrounding me, other sounds began to drift toward me. Something in the distance snorted, like a pig hunting for truffles, and a bird trilled high above me. The trees reached up into the sky, towering over me, their tops blending together too far away for me to make out clearly what else might be up there. My neck ached from staring too long so I turned my attention back to the task at hand and stepped lightly into the wild jungle.

It wasn't just the trees that had grown larger. Whatever fueled their change into this living, expanding, complex of branches and vines and trunks had encouraged the other plants too, and the animals were adapting to their new landscape. Mushrooms larger than my forearm grew, step-like, staggered up the sides of trees, and the ants that crawled around them were as long as my fingers. I glanced down at my boots to double check that my pants were tucked tightly into them. I'd made that mistake before, and still had faint scars on my left leg from bites that had gotten infected before they healed.

Leaves crunched under my feet as I moved slowly forward.

"Whee whee whee whee whee," trilled the birds. "Who who who who."

Birdsong and insect noises usually dropped off when a predator was nearby, so I moved faster, less worried about drawing attention to myself than I was about losing the already-fading light. The rifle strap rubbed against my chest, pushed the fabric of my tank top into my sweating skin as I climbed over exposed roots and ducked under low branches. I slipped once, grabbing for a vine to steady myself and ending up with a handful of hissing iguana instead. I'd pulled it from its perch, hadn't even seen the bastard, a huge specimen almost as long as I was. It wriggled violently, its back spines cutting into my hand, and I crushed its skull against a rock. It spasmed, and I slammed it down again and again until it stopped moving.

"Enough of this," I said to myself. "Time to try bait."

I pulled my knife free with my left hand and cut the lizard open in a small clearing, spilling its guts onto the ground. I cut its legs off with quick whacks, tossing them a few feet in each direction. "Doesn't that smell good, Mr. Monster?" I asked the wind as I wiped my blade on a flowering plant with huge blossoms redder than the iguana's blood. I stared at it for a moment, watching it stretch its leaves to catch the last of the sunlight, watching new tendrils unfurl.

Watching it grow right in front of me.

A rustle from across the clearing made me jump, drop my hand onto my pistol. I shook my head, clearing my thoughts, and pressed back against the jungle, hiding under a leafy tree I'd picked out moments before.

The rustling became rumbling.

I shook off a few too-curious ants and pulled my pistol free, holding it in both hands. I judged the distance too short to use the rifle effectively, and wanted the steadiest shot I could manage. I waited for the birds to stop chirping, for the air to still and the beast to come out into the open so I could kill it.

The brush exploded outward as a small herd of beasts rushed into view. I nearly shot the first one but held my breath and froze, taking in the scene. They were massive things, like cows but with snouts that moved wildly about, stubby tails and splayed feet. I struggled to remember what they were called but the images in my head of faded picture books didn't come with text. The big one at the front, grizzled and scarred, lifted its head to the sky and open its mouth wide, showing its blunt teeth as it snorted and sniffed the wind.

Tapirs, I thought. *They're tapirs.*

That'd make them herbivores, probably, and not the monster I was after. The big one put his face down, looking in my direction with cloudy blue eyes that probably saw very little. The others milled about, somehow satisfied that they weren't in danger—smaller animals I guess were females and even a spotted calf. It looked a little like a deer. Like Bambi, if his mother'd been a sow instead of a doe. A few ate gingerly from the leaves lowest to the ground, and a few others poked at the dead lizard parts but didn't eat. They were impressively large, like everything else in this place, mutated beyond their natural size. I relaxed and lowered my gun.

The birds stopped singing.

The biggest tapir's nose shot up into the air again, mouth hanging open. The others stopped milling around and moved nearer to him, their heads darting back and forth as if trying to catch the same scent. I looked too, seeing nothing. A delicate scent drifted in on the light breeze, and I struggled to identify it. The beasts smelled it too, their snouts rising. As one, they breathed slower, quieted. The daylight was almost gone. I wasn't sure if there was anything to be worried about anymore, and stopped thinking about the reason I'd come out here in the first place, but I was interested in what the tapirs were doing. It seemed strange to me, though I wasn't sure why. Holstering my pistol, I gently pulled my night-vision glasses from their reinforced case in my pocket. As thin as sunglasses, round like goggles, this little piece of technological advancement cost more than I made in a year and I was often hesitant to even pull them out.

Once on, the glasses snapped the animals into crisp green focus. They were still huddled together, though the sound of something coming closer to us was getting louder.

"Why don't you run?" I whispered.

The big one heard me. It shook its head, looking left and right. Its muscles shuddered under its smooth gray coat. Unsteadily, it walked into one of the females, as if drunk. She didn't move. *He must be the bull*, I thought, *the alpha male*, watching him shove her again. He leaned against her with his shoulder, knocking the smaller tapir over onto her side. She jumped up, shaking her head, and grunted at him. He repeated the action again with another female, grunting as he shouldered her to the ground. She too jumped up unsteadily, and together they broke the spell over the rest of their herd.

The scent of tart green apples filled the air.

I love apples.

My grandmother had an apple tree in the backyard. In the spring it would bloom such delicate flowers, and those flowers became tiny fruits, swelling as the days grew longer and warmer until they were ripe enough to pluck. My cousins and I would clamber into the tree like monkeys while Granny laughed from her back porch. She wore those flower-print aprons over her clothes, all day long, and we'd drop apples down to her that she'd catch in that faded fabric, held tight between wrinkled hands. She baked pies and fresh bread and every day that I went to visit her the sky was bright blue.

I stepped forward into the clearing.

I remember that I was smiling, thinking of apples.

That big tapir saved me. The others had scurried out of

the clearing while I pictured lemonade in cold glasses, chilled with real ice cubes. Granny had these tiny ice cube trays that made little ice, about half the size of standard cubes, perfect for crunching in the mouth of a child. She was so thoughtful that way. The tapir must have come back for me after his herd left because the next thing I knew the wind got knocked out of my lungs and I flew a couple of feet into the air before landing flat on my back. I coughed, struggling to suck in a breath. Not breathing cleared my head so I could see the monster for the first time.

The monster got my savior.

I don't know. It was big, so big, I'd never seen a cat like that. It must have been a jaguar at some point in its evolutionary history because it still had that yellow-black fur with black spots but it rippled when I looked at it. I tried to focus but all I could think about was being back in Arizona. It didn't even run, I don't know if it could, it was large. Bigger than a lion, or a tiger, it must have been 8 feet long.

My Granny used to make us cookies too, from scratch, with chunks of chocolate that she broke off from a bar and *the cat launched itself at the old herbivore and sank its teeth into the animal's neck* and there was this one time that a bunch of us packed up cookies and bottled water and those green apples *and the tapir screamed, its long nose wriggling as it struggled* and we went down to the river which still had water in it then and *the tapir sank to his knees and the monster that wouldn't hold its shape crunched through the tapir's neck and* we found all these baby tadpoles in the river and the sun was so bright *and the cat looked up at me with blood on its maw* and my cousin took a couple of them home and they turned out to be salamanders instead of frogs and I wanted one but my mom said no a water tank wouldn't be allowed in our building and *the cat walked toward me and* my Granny telling my father that I had to learn Spanish, I had to see Mexico, I had to know where I come from and Daddy yelling *and I think it's going to eat me next and*

    I shot it. I shot it and shot it and shot it until it was dead.

    After a while the smell of apples went away.

    The men came back, summoned by my tracking beacon, and by the time they'd arrived I'd cleared my head and started a rough examination of the creature. It was a jungle cat, of that I was sure, but one so large I think its mass would make it unable to maintain a killing burst of speed for more than a few seconds, if it even ran at all. Starting to smell of death and warm blood it lost its blur. The rumbling Jeep kept me from pondering it too much longer.

    "You didn't die!" Paco yelled from the front seat, jumping down before the engine died completely.

    "I'm glad you came," I said, pointing at the dead cat. "We're going to need a bigger Jeep." In the end we lashed it to the hood and leaned back as we drove to balance the weight. 15 miles an hour in the jungle on a beat-up dirt and gravel road meant 90 minutes of me unable to relax. If Paco noticed that I kept my reloaded pistol in my hand the whole ride back he didn't say anything. A shower and a fresh set of clothes later, I tucked my rifle back into its bag and headed out to meet the celebration.

    A poor village celebrating the death of a marauding monster is a hell of a place to be. Tequila flowed freely, candle lamps threw light and shadow across the pastel-painted walls, and the air was thick with the scent of sweat and cooking meat and lust and apples. Little children ran by laughing. They darted past smiling adults and stole sweets from the feast table and no one seemed to mind much. I had my boots up on a chair, a cold beer in my hand, and had just about finished my last round of "You're welcome, I'm just doing my job, de nada" when I saw that pink dress again.

God she was beautiful. A tiny smile on her face, dark brown eyes peering up at me. She was just a foot away and I nearly stopped breathing. I could have reached out and grabbed her right then.

She looked about six years old.

"Hello darling," I whispered. She stared at me but her pink lips never parted. "Do you want to come with me?" She didn't struggle as I led her away from the party. I glanced back but no one was looking for her.

"Where is your mama, little one?" I asked but she just smiled up at me. "Have I met your mama today? Is she in the village?" Nothing. We reached my room and she touched me, her little fingers pulling against my pant leg. I put a hand on her back, just below her neck, and pushed her gently into my room. Locking the door behind me, I turned to look at her.

"You're perfect, do you know that?" I sat on the bed, my head level with hers, and drew her close. She came to me. I sighed, breathing in the scent of sweetness and fruit and sugar. "Your hair, that dress, how could I resist you?"

She didn't answer.

I leaned in and licked her cheek. It felt smooth and the scent of her skin was overwhelming. I grabbed the back of her neck and she jerked at that but held still, staring with those huge eyes. I touched her lips with my free hand, softly stroking them, slipping a finger insider of her mouth. She bit me, hard enough to draw blood.

I slapped her hard and she fell to the ground with a hiss.

I looked at the blood welling up from the jagged teeth marks in my finger and sighed again. "I'm sorry, sweetie. I know, you're just a baby." I gathered her up, smoothed her hair, and nuzzled her neck until she calmed down. Laying her on the bed with me, I looked into those eyes one more time.

"You really are perfect. I've never seen anything quite like you. There was a little girl, looked like you, about two villages back, and I had to kill her too, but she wasn't so pretty. So pink and sweet." My hand was big enough to cover her mouth and nose at the same time, and I put my weight behind it, my leg across her body, and held her against me until the movement became silence and the smell of sweet treats faded away.

She never said a word.

Eventually my head cleared. I packed my bags. "This is going to be harder to explain, you know," I told her. "Paco doesn't recognize a monster when he sees one." Weapons, tech, one duffel bag—I ran over my checklist in my head, like I'd done a hundred times before, getting ready to leave this village and head out to the next one.

I took one last look at the bed, and the still figure on it, its black fur matted and its paws pulled in tight—and shook my head.

"I'm really starting to hate this job," I said, to no one in particular.

ABOUT THE MIRROR AND ITS PIECES

I was warmer when forgetting me was the way you broke my heart.

Green silk, white lace, red velvet at Christmas. My mother dressed me like a gift, wrapped me in bows, and set me out on the porch for you to find. Every fine dress I owned I wore, one after the other, waiting for you to come. I'm sure there must have been nights where you arrived on time because otherwise why would she have kept doing it? But I only know that I would sit on the steps, my tiny legs tucked under my skirts, wearing pretty toddler shoes that didn't quite fit, nothing to do but watch the cars drive past. Modesto doesn't freeze at night but by the time she decided I could come back inside I was usually stiff from sitting still, shivering, and up past my bedtime.

Waiting in the dark on the porch for a father who wasn't going to show.

It doesn't matter. You don't remember that, and neither do I. I only have the stories that my mother told me, and the vague sensation of cold concrete.

There were family reunions a couple of times a year. We'd drive through the night to get down to Sunnyvale, Acton, Venice Beach. Grandparents and aunts and cousins dressed in bright colors, my mother looking beautiful. She was always beautiful when she was happy. I watched her smiling, laughing, from my hiding spots. Under the table.

"Where's the weird girl?"

On the top stair.

"Who knows. She talks too fast anyway."

Behind the door of an unused bedroom.

"Her hands are cold. She touched me when we were playing tag and it was creepy."

A little girl can always find a way to be alone when no one is looking for her.

When I was eight I saw you again. Unexpectedly, without a word in my direction, I was bundled into another delicate dress and put into the car. By that age I was firmly into jeans and button down shirts, dirt-smudged sneakers and climbing into the big tree in the backyard. Dresses were for holidays and funerals but I owned one deemed good enough.

I had new sisters then, a trio of blond babies chasing after you. You were busy with one thing or another, something besides me. Your new wife entertained me instead. She fed me strawberry ice cream and tried to get me to smile, and I meant to, I really did, but the ice cream was cold and you didn't notice that I was there. The chill of it turned my mouth to snow. It slipped down my throat and into my belly and you walked right past the kitchen and...

You called me "dear" when I left.

"We'll see you soon, dear," and "Say goodbye to your sisters, dear," as if I'd get a chance to know them. As if I'd be invited back to your house next week for more ice cream, instead of waiting for you to remember me again. Year and years of waiting.

"What did you do?" my mother asked, a few months later. "Why doesn't anyone want you?"

I opened my mouth to answer but she'd already turned away. None of the words I meant to say formed into sounds. They fell out as wisps of frosty air instead. I said her name and watched it disappear as my breath warmed up to room temperature invisibility again.

That summer we went to the lake like we always did. The sun beat itself against the water sharply, cutting back across the sides of the house boat, flashing across my mother and her friends. I sat with my feet dangling over the edge, toes making tiny waves as the boat moved slowly along. The water felt wet but not cold, not any colder than I already was.

I didn't notice the sun baking me bright red.

"How are you the only person in our family who doesn't tan?" my mother asked as she smeared aloe across my shoulders. We'd gone into the cabin, out of the sun. "Stay inside and read a book or something. You can't go back in the water this weekend." She sighed, her breath hot on my back. "Does it hurt?"

I shook my head, the ends of my hair catching in the thick goo smeared on my skin. She sighed again, pulling the strands out and twisting my hair up into a pony tail.

"Try not to move much. I'll come check on you in a few hours." She stood, frowning. "I think you're actually getting paler. You really need to get outside more often."

I thought of all the time I spent outside already. I made a list to tell her about— playground swings, backyard tree, reading books on the couch on the front porch in the afternoon—until the splashing and laughing reminded me she'd already gone.

I just now realized that you never called me by my name.

We went to the mountains for a vacation one winter.

"I'm tired of dragging you around," she said. "You never want to have any fun. You can just play outside and be miserable by yourself." I had never seen snow in a quantity greater than the sometimes frost that turned the grass white in January so I watched out the window as the ground rose and the fields gave way to mountains. Green became speckled with white, then covered by it. The dirt and trash and everything got covered up by a blanket of perfection.

Inside the A-frame cabin, owned by other friends of hers, there was a fireplace and I remember the sound of ice tinkling against glass while someone told jokes and everyone laughed. I don't know who. Someone's husband or boyfriend—I could never keep track of all my mother's friends. Too warm in there and too crowded and no one would notice me slipping out through the sliding glass door, so I did.

The night was quiet, empty, and cool. I laid in the snow and watched the stars come out, blossoming in the darkness. When the moon rose the yard lit up, reflecting the moonlight like a million tiny shards of mirror.

> It turns out that snow is beautiful.
> Did you know that?

When I was sixteen, you came for me. One day I was in school and you were there, in the back of the class. The teacher introduced you to the class, and until that moment I hadn't realized who you were. You told my mother later that everyone mistook you for my boyfriend. I don't know how they could have, you were three times my age.

In your head that was better, I guess, than being my father.

We sat on the couch, the three of us, my parents and I, watching television as if this was a thing we did every night. Your hand rested on my leg, under the blankets, and I didn't think much of it then. It was a small spot of warmth on skin gone cold years ago. It was the gentle touch of someone who should have been there for me all along.

It was comfortable. For a moment I felt safe.

It was a mistake not to see that you would take it as permission. It didn't occur to me at the time.

"My own daughter's getting hot for me," you said in the car as we drove, us two, up to Oregon where you were living at the time. I looked out the window as the highway took me farther from home.

"You have great breasts," you'd said. "Like baseballs. My mother had breasts like yours."

I didn't know what any of it meant, so I rolled down the glass and let the cold air wash over me.

"Come here," you said, dragging my by the wrist toward the bedroom as if it were a casual request and not an order enforced by your insistence and the foot of height you had over me. And, later, whispered, sometime in the middle of it all, "What else are darling daughters for?"

I didn't answer.

I don't know.

I bit my lip to keep from screaming, closed my eyes against the sight of you, and buried myself in the snow inside my chest to keep from feeling anything at all. I was trapped there, you said. Unwanted, you said. Things had changed and I had better get used to it. What choice did I have?

But that was a lie too. You were done with me in a week and sent me back home to my mother.

"Have you seen your report card?" she asked me the following winter. "You're failing PE, won't participate. Cs and

D everywhere else, won't participate. Won't talk in class." She pulled her cardigan closed, shivering against a chill I didn't notice. "You need to keep your bedroom windows closed. You'll freeze to death in here." I nodded and slid the glass nearest to me shut.

"You're so pale. And could you at least pretend to smile? If you fail out of school and you're miserable all of the time, no one is going to want you. You're not staying here forever, do you hear me?"

I opened the window again when she'd gone.

Eventually there wasn't a place for me in my mother's house anymore. I went back to the mountains, tried college, and made it through a year before my reputation grew loud enough that even I could hear it. "That girl doesn't say no," the boys said. "If you just pull her into bed she won't say anything at all."

Can't argue against a rumor when it's true.

I sat on a bench outside of some class or another, sitting for hours as the sun set and the temperature dropped and no one asked me what was wrong. Students walked by, going with some purpose to the next place they had to be. The cafeteria, and then the library, closed behind me. The distant sounds of normal campus life faded into silence.

By morning I had moved on to somewhere new.

When I was twenty-four I called you on the phone. The plastic chilled as I pushed the buttons, one number after another, dialing your new wife's house. Not the one from when I was a child, the one that would come after, who was only a decade older than me. I don't know why I did it, and as I sat listening to your drug-addled voice telling me how you'd been to the dentist that day and by the way, what did I want? My voice froze completely. I breathed out tiny flakes of ice instead of words and eventually you hung up.

Eventually I couldn't stay in California any more. The fake smile on my lips hurt, cracking my cheeks open on the inside, and no one understood why I was always cold. They would crawl into bed with me for my beauty, find a way to warm themselves under the sheets, and crawl back out again complaining of my frozen hands, frozen feet. Frozen heart.

Too many to remember. What does it matter, anyway?

In the summer months, when the temperature shot up, the heat made me sick. Sun hot, oven hot, drying dying desert hot air pressed against my skin and the ice in my veins pressed back. I couldn't live that way.

I moved East instead, and when I found that the depth of winter was cold enough to soothe my skin and settle my stomach, I moved again, further North. Looking for the right amount of ice.

These days I live in a place where it snows every day, so no one notices how cold I am. We all wear thick jackets, wooly gloves, knitted scarves twined round and round our necks. When I breathe out frozen wisps of air, so does everyone else. I don't stand out here.

No one notices that it snows when I cry. I do cry, still, slow teardrops dripping down my cheeks, or great howling sobs racking my chest. You'd think I wouldn't by now but this ache never goes away. My voice carries out into the world as the howl of a storm. If life were any kind of fair there would be at least one person who cared that I hurt so much ...

No one asks what's wrong with me, and that is better, I

think, than having to pretend that nothing's broken, nothing's lost. I see people each time I leave my home but I don't think they see me. We walk past each other in the city square, swaddled against the chill, smiling without looking at each other, really. Between the snow and my skin and silence I wonder—if I dressed all in white would anyone notice me at all?

Some days I think that if I had a child, I would be warm again. A little laughing voice to fill the rooms of my house. A warm body snuggled under blankets with me, books of brightly colored stories, little ice skates, little boots. He could play outside in the snow and when he got cold he would come into the kitchen and I would make him hot chocolate and dry him with a fluffy towel and he would be warm again. I'd name him Kay, or Kai, or one of those happy, sunny names. Or something solid, like Edmund, so he'd be sure to stay by my side, instead of blowing away on the winter wind.
I'll know him when I see him. I'll name him then.
Of course I would have a son. I'd have to.
I wouldn't know what to do with a daughter.

ABOUT THE STORIES

"Mrs. Henderson's Cemetery Dance", originally published in *Red Penny Papers*, Summer 2012

A dead guy looking for his arm. That's what I had in my head at first, and nothing else. Okay, so why is he looking for his arm? Who took it? Who would? Well, a hungry dog might dig up a corpse, and then run off with the bit it could fit in its mouth... but that's not a dignified way for said corpse to spend his eternal rest, and just the right sort of person might be offended enough to get up and do something about it.

On a rewrite I named all of the characters after people I knew—friends, fellow writers, and relatives (loved and unloved)—except for Mary, the Herbert's daughter. Her father was an old friend of mine, sort of nearly a boyfriend once upon a time, but I have no idea if he has any children now.

"Letter From A Murderous Construct and His Robot Fish", written August 2011

We'll call it a dare. I made a few comments on Twitter late one night, got some encouragement from Ken Liu, and found myself writing a Shakespearean sonnet which had to include robots, a fish, and a murder. Putting all of that into 14 lines, and making sure the right parts rhymed...
It was a challenge. I'm not sure I won it.

"Annabelle Tree", originally published in *Southern Fried Weirdness: Reconstruction*, May 2011

I had an idea for a tale about a young girl whose only

friend was the tree growing in her yard, but I didn't sit down to write it until I saw the anthology call for submissions. TJ McIntyre, who I knew from various places around the Internet (and who I later published in *FISH*, which I edited for Dagan Books) was collecting stories for a charity anthology that would raise money for the American Red Cross. He hoped the book would help survivors of a recent string of tornadoes.

It was the tornado that told me how to finish the story, and knowing the end got me started.

"A Cage, Her Arms", written April 2013

When you have a child, you often think that in your arms, surrounded by your love, is the best and safest place they can be, but at some point you have to let them grow into who they are. Even if that means you no longer understand them.

"Call Center Blues", originally published in *Daily Science Fiction*, November 2011

I was working in a call center for an educational testing company, the kind that makes the tests you need to take to get into college. (Yes, that test. And yes, that one too.) In between calls I started scribbling out notes for what would become "Call Center Blues". I wrote the entire thing in one day, ran it through a couple of edits and submitted it to *Daily Science Fiction*. A few weeks later I had my first pro-rate fiction sale.

Plus I got to use a *Twilight Zone* homage in this story, which delights my TZ-loving heart to no end.

"Mitch's Girl", originally published in *Rigor Amortis*, October 2010

Getting into the mind-set of a country boy with dead-girl tastes required repeat listenings of a soundtrack I created just for this story:

- Laura Veirs's "July Flame" invoked those last summer evenings, when the corn is ripe and the sky is darkening to a deeper shade of blue. It's a song for sitting quietly on the porch, a cool drink and a cotton dress.
- "Simple Man" by Lynyrd Skynyrd has that long slow sound which reminds me that nothing needs to be rushed. Lyrically, it's a song about being a good person with simple, down home, values, but musically it has a melodic tension in the bass line which stretches out over a faster guitar track, like pulling molasses out of a jar.
- The Me First and the Gimmie Gimmie's cover of "Country Roads" reminds me of being in the passenger seat of a truck driven by a boy I didn't know well enough to be driving with, one of my feet up on the dashboard, singing loudly to the original of this song while taking the curves of a winding mountain road just a little too fast. It reminds me of high summer, yellowing grasses, and a dry heat in the afternoon.
- "Cross-Eyed Mary" by Jethro Tull brings me the creepy factor I needed for the this story. The lyrics are dark and wanting, and the singer lends his dirty secrets to the song when he sings. I needed all of that, and a bit more, to write about longing for a response from a woman who only exists from the navel down.

"All The Right Words", originally published in *Goldfish Grimm*, March 2012

I defend genre writing when the inevitable complaints about plotting and characters come up. Too often people think that adding a science fiction or fantasy element makes the writer rely on the special effects instead of telling a story. I always try to write a story which would make perfect sense in our world, even though I've set it in someone else's.

"All The Right Words" took the classic cheating husband/lying boyfriend conflict off-world, but still retains all of the elements we'd recognize from tabloid romances and our own personal heartbreaks.

"Monsters, Monsters, Everywhere," originally published in *Crossed Genres Magazine*, December 2011

It's July of 2011, and I'm driving in my car with Don Pizarro and Eric Rosenfield, taking Eric back to the train station after a long and happy Readercon. We're talking about weird food, and I admitted to once trying cat while on a vacation in Mexico (it was the 80s, we were in a tiny coastal village, and I was the kind of adventurous that comes from being a teenager not experienced enough to know better—I tried iguana on that trip, too). I've since had shark a couple of times, an ostrich burger in Davis, CA, and alligator gumbo in New Orleans, but the cat was too strange for me to repeat.

That same weekend, Kay Holt from *Crossed Genres* had asked me to submit a story to her magazine. I had no idea what I wanted to write about, but I liked the idea of writing something for CG. The deadline for the "Monsters" issue was coming up fast...

On the long drive home from Boston, those two pieces of information—this deadline and my culinary flashback—blended together to start me writing on "Monsters, Monsters,

Everywhere". After some back and forth with the editors, the original *gato* meal became spicy *cabra* (goat) meat instead. While it is just as good with that change, without the cat there'd have been no story in the first place, which goes to show that you should always start the story you mean to write, even if you turn it into something else later.

"About the Mirror and its Pieces", written February 2013

This story was meant to push the boundaries of fiction by mixing together some of my childhood with the imagined back story of the Snow Queen. She's a villain in the Hans Christian Anderson story, and in C.S. Lewis's *Narnia* tales, but I've always wondered how she got that way.

Maybe she started out as a little girl, the way the rest of us do, without any evil in her heart at all.

Made in the USA
Lexington, KY
13 July 2013